THE GOLD MINER'S GHOST

by John Sazaklis   Illustrated by Christian Cornia

PICTURE WINDOW BOOKS
a capstone imprint

Published by Picture Window Books, an imprint of Capstone
1710 Roe Crest Drive, North Mankato, Minnesota 56003
capstonepub.com

Library of Congress Cataloging-in-Publication Data
Names: Sazaklis, John, author. | Cornia, Christian, 1975- illustrator.
Title: The gold miner's ghost / by John Sazaklis ;
illustrated by Christian Cornia.
Description: North Mankato, Minnesota : Picture Window Books, an
imprint of Capstone, [2021] | Series: Scooby-Doo! mini mysteries |
Audience: Ages 5–7. | Audience: Grades K–1. |
Summary: The Mystery Inc. gang visits a guest ranch
that is haunted by an old prospector.
Identifiers: LCCN 2021002768 (print) | LCCN 2021002769 (ebook) |
ISBN 9781663909947 (hardcover) | ISBN 9781663921260 (paperback) |
ISBN 9781663909916 (ebook pdf)
Subjects: CYAC: Mystery and detective stories. | Ghosts—Fiction. |
Lost and found possessions—Fiction. | Great Dane—Fiction. |
Dogs—Fiction. Classification: LCC PZ7.S27587 Go 2021 (print) |
LCC PZ7.S27587 (ebook) | DDC [E]—dc23
LC record available at https://lccn.loc.gov/2021002768
LC ebook record available at https://lccn.loc.gov/2021002769

Design Element: Shutterstock: klyaksun

Designer: Tracy Davies

Printed and bound in the USA. 4270

TABLE OF CONTENTS

MEET THE MYSTERY INC. GANG!

SHAGGY

Norville "Shaggy" Rogers is a laid-back dude who would rather search for food than clues . . . but he usually finds both!

SCOOBY-DOO

A happy hound with a super snout, Scooby-Doo is the mascot of Mystery Inc. He'll do anything for a Scooby Snack!

FRED

Fred Jones, Jr. is the oldest member of the group. Friendly and fun-loving, he's a good sport—and good at them too.

DAPHNE

Brainy and bold, the fashion-forward Daphne Blake solves mysteries with street smarts and a sense of style.

VELMA

Velma Dinkley is clever and book smart. She may be the youngest member of the team, but she's an old pro at cracking cases.

MYSTERY MACHINE

Not only is this van the gang's main way of getting around, but it is stocked with all the equipment needed for every adventure.

CHAPTER ONE

RANCH RACE

The Mystery Inc. gang was headed to the Gold City Guest Ranch.

"Tonight we are living the pioneer life of the Old West," said Daphne.

"Like, as long as the food is not old," Shaggy said.

"Rhat's right!" Scooby-Doo agreed.

Just then, a spooky, bearded figure
staggered out of a cave and into the
road. It moaned loudly and leaped
toward the van!

"ZOINKS!" Shaggy exclaimed.

"Ret's get out of here!" added Scooby.

Fred swerved around the spooky figure and took another road.

Up ahead, the terrified teens saw the ranch. Big Ben, the owner, came out to greet them.

"Are you okay?" he asked.

"Like, we may have seen a ghost!" said Shaggy.

"It just happens to be our luck," added Daphne.

"Well, I've had nothing but bad luck," Ben said. "All the gold in the local mine has gone missing."

"RUH-ROH!" Scooby yelped.

CHAPTER TWO

CAVE CREEP

Inside the inn, the gang met Hank, the caretaker.

"Beware the Miner Forty-Niner!" he warned. "That 200-year-old prospector haunts the hills."

"Stop it, Hank! You'll scare our guests away," Big Ben said.

"No need to fear," replied Fred.
"We are the members of Mystery Inc.
Solving mysteries is our job."

"We will save the day during our
stay!" added Velma.

Later that night, Daphne and Velma heard a loud moan outside their room.

The girls followed the sound. It was the Miner Forty-Niner!

"JEEPERS!" Daphne screamed.

The miner disappeared as Daphne and Velma rushed out of their room. They rammed right into Shaggy and Scoob.

SMASH!

Snacks scattered everywhere.

"Like, what's the hurry?" Shaggy asked. "Are you hungry too?"

"We just saw the miner outside our room," Daphne said.

"He disappeared, but he dropped this map first," Velma said.

They found Fred and followed the map to the gold mine. Loud moaning echoed through the caves.

Scooby hid behind Shaggy, who hid behind the others.

"Let's go get that gold-digging ghoul!" Fred said.

"Not before I get you!" howled Miner Forty-Niner.

"ZOINKS!" Shaggy shouted. "He's one step ahead of us!"

"The map led us to a trap!" said Velma.

Miner Forty-Niner chased the frightened friends. The gang tried to escape down a mine shaft. But the ghost grabbed Scooby-Doo.

"Relp!" Scooby yelled.

CHAPTER THREE

FOOL'S GOLD

The gang stumbled through a dark tunnel. They came upon a track near a mine cart.

"**GROOVY!**" said Fred. "A new set of wheels."

"We can use the cart to get away from that ghost," Daphne said.

"Scooby-Doo, where are you?"

Shaggy called.

AROOOOOOOO!

Just then, Scooby leaped out of the shadows. But he was not alone.

The Miner Forty-Niner was right on his tail!

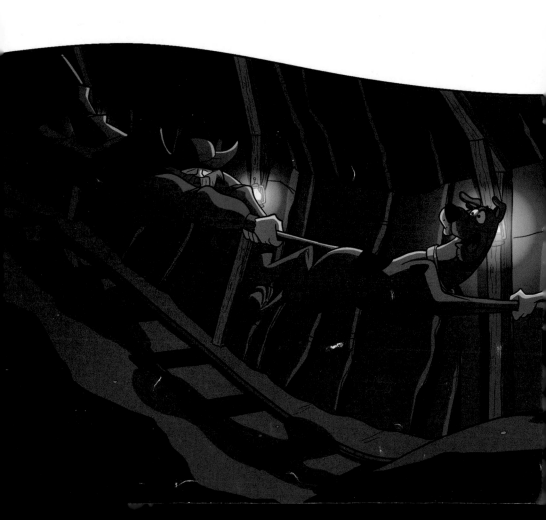

WHOOSH!

The mine cart streaked downhill with rocket-like speed. At the end of the track, the cart tipped. It threw everybody out. They landed in a secret cave hideout.

The cart landed right on top of the moaning miner. His hat and beard came off to reveal Hank the caretaker!

"**JINKIES!**" Velma said. "The ghost is a grumpy old gold-digger."

"Look!" Daphne said. "All of Big Ben's stolen gold was hidden in here."

"This gold would have been all mine!" Hank hollered. "If not for you meddling kids and that pesky pup!"

"Like, this miner is just a big whiner," Shaggy said.

The police took Hank away, and the gold was returned to Big Ben. The gang headed to the saloon for a victory snack.

"I love the way of life in the old west," Fred said.

"With our adventures, it's more like the wild west," Daphne replied.

Scooby agreed.

"SCOOBY-DOOBY-DOO!"

GLOSSARY

ghoul—ghost

meddling—to interfere with someone else's business

pesky—troublesome

pioneer—a person who is one of the first to try new things

prospector—a person who looks for valuable minerals, especially silver and gold

saloon—a type of restaurant

shaft—a passage that goes through the floors of a building

AUTHOR

John Sazaklis is a *New York Times* best-selling author with almost 100 children's books under his utility belt! He has also illustrated Spider-Man books, created toys for *MAD* magazine, and written for the BEN 10 animated series. John lives in New York City with his superpowered wife and daughter.

ILLUSTRATOR

Christian Cornia is a character designer, illustrator, and comic artist from Modena, Italy. He has created artwork for publishers, advertisers, and video games. He currently teaches character design at the Scuola Internazionale di Comics of Reggio Emilia. Christian works digitally but remains a secret lover of the pencil, and he doesn't go anywhere without a sketchbook in his bag.

TALK ABOUT IT

1. Life in the Old West days was a lot different from how you live now. What do you think was different?

2. Do you think it was a good idea for the gang to follow the map they found? Why or why not?

3. Were you surprised that the Miner Forty-Niner was actually caretaker Hank? Explain your answer.

WRITE ABOUT IT

1. Make a list of three ways to get people to come back to Gold City now that the ghost is gone.

2. The Mystery Inc. gang has lots of adventures. Write a story about an adventure that you have had.

3. Pick a favorite illustration from the story. Write about why you like it.

Help solve mystery after mystery
with Scooby-Doo and the gang!

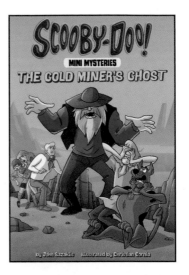

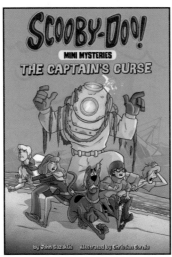

NEW TITLES!